Monacello

THE LITTLE MONK

Written by Geraldine McCaughrean
Illustrated by Jana Diemberger

MONACELLO - The Little Monk

ISBN: 978-1-907912-03-0

Published in Great Britain by Phoenix Yard Books Ltd

This edition published 2011

Phoenix Yard Books
Phoenix Yard
65 King's Cross Road
London
WC1X 9LW

1 3 5 7 9 10 8 6 4 2

Set in Caslon and Caslon Antique

Book design by Insight Design Concepts

Printed in China

A CIP catalogue record for this book is available from the British Library

www.phoenixyardbooks.com

Monacello

THE LITTLE MONK

Written by Geraldine McCaughrean
Illustrated by Jana Diemberger

CHAPTER ONE

ONLY A BABY

It all began with a knock at the door and no one there, only a crate half-filled with straw. The nuns who came to the door of the convent hoped it might be a gift of fruit or eggs or bread. But no … it was only a baby.

Only a baby? Who finds a baby smelling of warm bread, fragile as eggs, and says, "Only a baby?"

"Oh dear," said the nun who uncovered the little yellow face.

"Not right," said the nun

who unparcelled the tiny body. Beneath its tiny body lay two pieces of cloth; one black and one red.

"The colours of sin and darkness," said a third. "A creature of wickedness, surely. Everything God makes is perfect."

But Sister Clementa simply picked up the baby and cuddled him.

"Nonsense," she said. "Nobody's perfect."

Day by day and night by night, she washed and rocked the baby.

The others only complained about his crying. The two pieces of cloth she folded under his head for a pillow: one side red, one side black.

When he began to walk, she made him a robe of dark wool and called him Little Monk: Monacello.

"More monkey than monk," said the other nuns and sent him out into the yard where they would not have to look at him.

Beyond the gates of the convent, children of the same age grew tall and strong, but Monacello barely grew at all. Ugly and squat, he reminded the nuns of the gargoyles that jutted from the bell tower.

"At least he will not grow out of his clothes," said Sister Clementa brightly. "And just look at that smile!"

Monacello did not grow out of his clothes, but he did grow out of his smile.

That Christmas, he heard stories about the baby Jesus (who was also found in a box of straw, by the way) and Jesus' mother, Mary.

"Are you my mother?" he asked Sister Clementa, but she only laughed and shook her head.

He asked every nun in the convent, "Are you my
mother?" But each clapped a hand to her cheek —
"Certainly not!" — and told him he was a fool.

He began to search in earnest for his mother. He looked
under all the beds, scattering sandals and chamber pots.
He looked in the laundry, emptying clean linen on to the

dirty floor. He looked in the larder, spilling the rice in a
hissing stream. The nuns called him "Pest!" "Nuisance!"
and "Mischief!" But he found no sign of
his mother.

At night the nuns complained that there were owls in
the outhouse. But it was only Monacello, crying for his
lost mother. By day they complained there were cats in
the chapel. But it was only Monacello whimpering as he

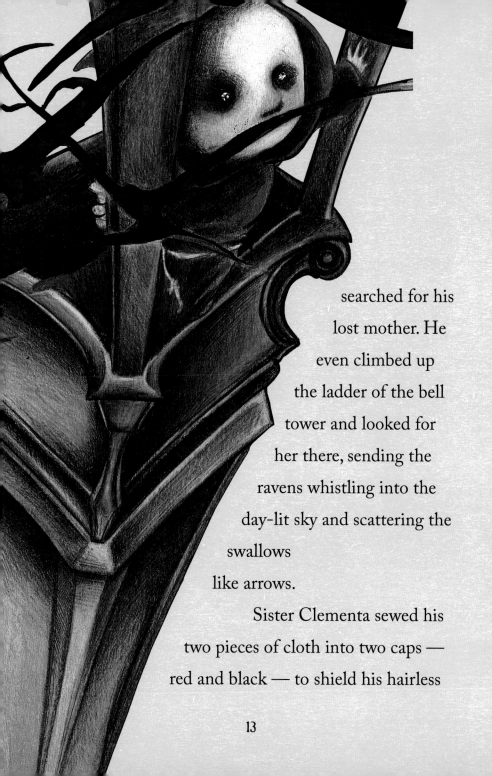

searched for his
lost mother. He
even climbed up
the ladder of the bell
tower and looked for
her there, sending the
ravens whistling into the
day-lit sky and scattering the
swallows
like arrows.

Sister Clementa sewed his
two pieces of cloth into two caps —
red and black — to shield his hairless

13

head from sun and snow. Some days he wore red, some days he wore black. Often, though, neither showed, because Monacello began to wear his monk's hood up, to hide his face.

Glimpsing his small shadow scurrying along the dark cloisters, the nuns caught their breath in fright: such a snuffling, scuttling, scuffling little creature; goblin-strange.

"Out of here! Out!" they cried, "Out of here, you ugly little boy!" and flapped their black robes at him.

"Ugly? Is that what I am?" thought Monacello, and put on "ugly" like another little dark robe.

CHAPTER TWO

LOOKING FOR MOTHER

When he could not find his mother inside the nunnery, he went outside into the street. Tottering along on his little legs, he looked under every cart and in all the shop doorways. He looked at the face of every woman who went by, and the women drew in their skirts, because Monacello's pale and peering eyes scared them.

"Go away. Go away, ugly boy!" they said, and flicked their shawls at him. But he went on looking.

He tipped up the empty barrels outside the inn, to look underneath, and sent them booming and barrelling down the street. People scattered to right and left. Horses bolted. Fists shook.

The children playing in the streets stopped to watch and laugh as the barrels went bowling by. When Monacello toddled into sight, they blinked at him. Perhaps they were afraid, because they drew together into a pack, white teeth glittering as they jeered and sneered.

"What are you? A mushroom in a frock?"

"Nah, look, he's all brown. Must be a rat!"

"Whatever he is, let's get him!"

Monacello ran, dodging between the legs of the shoppers in the market and, when the children came after him, he crept under the long table of a butcher's stall. A flurry of flies rose off the joints of meat. The darkness under the table was full of bones and offal and puddles of blood. There was certainly no mother for Monacello under there, only the clutter of kicking feet and the angry roar of the butcher.

Somehow the trestles got knocked. The table tilted. The meat slid — SPLAT! — on to the ground. Suddenly every dog in Naples appeared from nowhere, and ran off with meat in its grinning mouth.

And in among the dogs ran Monacello. For a while the shouts came after him, then faded away into silence.

"Do you know where I can find my mother?" he asked, but the dogs spoke their own language. Anyway, their legs were longer and they outran him.

CHAPTER THREE

BAD LUCK BOY

That is how he came to the gates of the Villa Frezza. The spikes on the gate were sharp as spears. The house beyond had been beautiful once, with periwinkles clambering up the walls and little balconies painted gold. But the flowers had died and the paint had peeled, so now the house looked old, wrinkled and veiny. The gutters sagged like angry eyebrows.

An old man on the balcony scowled, too, when he saw Monacello's face pushed between the railings. Pointing a wavering finger, baring his teeth, Old Man Frezza threw a flowerpot that smashed against the spiky gates.

Further down the hill stood a row of barns. Crates packed with straw were stacked as high as the roof; in them the treasure that had made Old Man Frezza rich — velvety peaches, apples, grapes, purple plums, freckled eggs and wild strawberries. These the Frezza family sold at market, to people who lived in the dark, stony and treeless streets of Naples.

Monacello meant
no mischief, he was
only scuffling by,
but all of a sudden
"Ow! Oh!"
They were not
luscious peaches or
apples that hit him,
but pulpy plums and a
sludge of rotten strawberries. Monacello

20

ran, tripping and
slipping on the slime.
"Oh! Ow!" Along with mushy
grapes and rotten eggs, the Frezza boys
threw unkind words sharper than peach stones: "Devil!"
"Goblin" "Gremlin!" "Demon!"

For the first time (but not the last) Monacello's pale
eyes flashed dark with anger. "Demon, am I?" he thought.

Behind him, a tower of crates came crashing down.

After dark, he went back to the nunnery, but the gates were locked, the shutters shut. The vespers bell tolled for evening prayers, but not for the Little Monk. Candlelight poked out through the shutters like yellow straw in a crate, but it did not fall on Monacello. He was shut out in the dark.

Next morning, the stall in the market was selling fruit as usual. But the apples were bruised, the plum skins were split and the green beans were snapped. When the customers complained, so too did the boy serving.

"A stack of crates fell … It's the fault of that little demon Monacello," he said. "One look from him brings Bad Luck!"

"It does?" said his customers.

"It does," said the Frezza boy.

Suddenly a woman remembered seeing the Little Monk walk under her washing line just before the washing blew down into the mud. "Had to wash it all over again," said the woman.

"Bad luck," said the boy, nodding.

A widow remembered how she had found the child stroking her goat. "Next time I milked her, the milk was sour!"

"Bad luck," said another Frezza boy, joining his brother behind the fruit stall. "That will be Monacello."

"Saw that goblin yesterday, then the cat ate my supper!" The woman did not blame the cat, she blamed Monacello.

"My sweetheart ran away to sea," said a tearful girl. "It's all that monkey's fault!" She did not blame her sweetheart, but Monacello, bringer of Bad Luck.

After that, if people saw a scuffling little figure in a dark woollen robe, they drew away, scared of Bad Luck. Sometimes they picked up rubbish to throw, shouted threats to frighten him away, or called on the saints to protect them from Bad Luck Boy, Monacello.

"Is that what I am? Bad luck?" thought Monacello.

"All right, then … that's what I'll be." And he put on Bad Luck like one more black and itchy robe.

He opened garden gates so that goats would stray, cut washing lines, filled locks with mud, knocked on doors and ran away. Monacello hoped it would make him laugh, like other children laughed. And sure enough, when he caught sight of his reflection, there was a smirk on his face. He looked just like those grinny dogs that had stolen the butcher's meat.

Monacello got the blame for many things he did not do. When Signora Trascurata could not find her mixing spoon, she said, "Monacello must have stolen it."

When Signor Basette lost his packed lunch he said, "Monacello must have been hungry."

What did it feel like to be Master of Mischief? A little bit exciting, fizzy and hot: What shall I get up to today? But each night the fizz fizzled away for Monacello.

Then he curled up in a doorway, like one of the cats who prowled the city at night. The midnight cats licked the stains out of Monacello's robe and the grape pips out of his wispy hair. He looked almost washed and brushed by the time the cats were done with him.

Naples had a lot of cats and Monacello liked every one of them. Sometimes he roamed the city alongside them, balancing along window sills and roof ridges, skittering over the bridges and through the empty market squares, gobbling up garbage and chasing rats.

He gave them names — Wormy, Fleahouse, Hairdrop — and the cats loved him for it. No one had given them anything as nice as names before.

Monacello slept under a mountain of cats.

CHAPTER FOUR

THE FREZZAS

The cats hunted mice and rats through the drains and rubbish dumps.

The Frezza family hunted the Little Monk.

For no reason that Monacello could see, they came after him with fists and stones. They came after him with clubs and big dogs. "Death to Monacello!" "Death to the goblin!"

"What bad luck I must have brought them!" thought Monacello as he ran for his life. Luckily, the cats showed him secret places to hide.

But one day he was busy playing a trick, and he did not see the brothers coming …

The Frezza boys chased him up the hills and down the lanes. They chased him through the fish market and along the waterfront. They chased him through narrow streets where families shouted from their balconies: "Get him!" "Catch him, the Bad Luck boy!"

At last Monacello jumped up on to the wall of a well, while Frezza dogs boiled and moiled all around, foam between their teeth.

Strange little creature. Strange pale eyes, so full of fear. Strange little monk, his habit as dark

as nightmares. Strange little boy, shaped like a question mark: Who are you?

"He's nothing but a little boy," said a woman in a sky-blue shawl, at the front of the crowd. "Leave him be."

But a Frezza took off his boot and threw it. Monacello fell like a bird down a chimney, down into the deep dark well. He fell without a cry: motherless Monacello, unloved as a kitten drowned in a bucket.

Next day, the water from the well tasted bitter. No one could drink it without pulling an ugly face.

CHAPTER FIVE

THE UNDERCITY

At the bottom of the well — SPLASH! — Monacello, blind in the dark, grasped and struggled to keep afloat. But he sank.

Boys drown who fall into wells, don't they?

Monacello reached out a hand and felt only the smooth slime of the well wall.

Down and down he sank.

"Monacello is dead! The Bad Luck boy is dead!" the Frezza boys crowed, whooping through the streets. People clapped. The boys decorated their fruit stall with ribbons and scarves.

Down and down he sank…. Until his reaching hand felt a hole in the well wall, and beyond the hole, a drain.

At the bottom of the well lay a maze of waterways spreading out like the roots of a tree, watering the roots of the city. At the bottom of the well lay something even more wonderful.

The Undercity!

Naples is an ancient city. The centuries have piled it up like the chapters in a book, one city on top of the one before. Underneath Naples-in-the-Sunshine lies Naples-in-the-Dark.

Here, once, Romans in togas and sandals cooked and worked, ate and slept, painted their walls with pictures, paved their floors with coloured stones, while the river flowed outside their windows and fruit trees grew in their sunny courtyards. Now the windows had no view but darkness; the courtyards had no sky but the floors and streets above them.

This is where Monacello found himself: little monk

bumped and bruised; little monk shivering in his wet clothes; little monk in the dark.

But he was not alone.

The Undercity hid many secrets. Ghosts and rats … and even friends.

"Wormy! Fleahouse! Hairdrop!"

The cats showed Monacello passageways to everywhere, secrets stairs into the cellars and crypts overhead, wriggling roundabout routes up to the sunlight. Monacello made his home in a room where painted grapes grew across the broken wall.

He still came and went, up into the sunlight, up into the starlight, searching for his mother, making mischief, stealing candles, folding bad news into paper darts to throw at city windows.

And now the people were much more afraid.

"Monacello is dead! The Bad Luck boy is dead!" the Frezza boys had crowed, whooping through the streets.

Why then did the Widow Casseruola see a dark little shape in her garden the day her hen stopped laying? What was that flicker of movement the blacksmith saw out of the corner of his eye just before he was kicked by a horse? Why did it rain before the housepainter's paint was dry? Why did the Bad Luck not come to an end? Who could it be, then, that dark shape half-seen? A goblin? A ghost? A gremlin?

Fearing bad luck, the people left out little presents to bribe the shadowy shape. "Go away!" said the presents.

"Well!" thought Monacello in astonishment. "You're scared of me now, are you? Am I frightening?" And he put on "frightening" like yet another dark scratchy robe, and took his presents home to the house with the tainted grapes.

CHAPTER SIX

KING OF THE UNDERCITY

The King of the Undercity, Monacello, sat among his presents with the cats at his feet.

"Hairdrop, you can be my Chancellor. Wormy, you are Lord Mayor. Fleahouse, you must protect my treasure." There was a post for every cat and kitten: Prime Minister, Ambassador, Chief of Police, Head Cook and Admiral. (The littlest kitten did not get a job, because it was curled up asleep in Monacello's red cap.)

"I'm rich now," declared Monacello … though he did not feel very rich.

Actually, I'm lonely, he thought, but not out loud, of course, as it would have hurt the cats' feelings. He just slipped into "lonely", like yet another damp, dark robe and felt his teeth chatter.

That night, his roaming took him to a magnificent church, in search of candles to steal. A thousand candles juggled a thousand golden flames as an organ played. Sweet-smelling smoke hung purple in the air and moonlight puddled the floor with silver. The candlelight snagged in his eyelashes. He opened his mouth in amazement and his tongue tasted … wonder!

There was a woman in a sky-blue dress. Of course, it was only a statue. Monacello knew that. Still, he could not help asking: "Are you my mother?"

"Of course not," said a voice behind him. "I'm Napolina."

Monacello spun round. There, like a heap of rags on the floor, lay a little girl. Her face was pointy like a rat, but Monacello liked rats. (You cannot live in the Undercity without liking rats.) Her clothes were sewn from the rags of a dozen garments: a sleeve, a collar, a shawl, a knitted stocking, a hood, an apron string … though over her heart was a patch of sky-blue cloth.

Her eyes were pale, like his, but the sadness in them was all her own and as deep as any well.

"Hello, Monacello," she said.

"You know my name?"

"The cats told me."

And suddenly Monacello saw that his Ambassador, Head Cook and the Chief of Police, his Chancellor, Admiral and Treasurer had all followed him into the church. Their fur silver with moonlight, eyes full of candlelight, they prowled the rails and ledges, the benches and sills.

The bang of a door, a cruel wind, and out went all the candles. In came a priest and, seeing the cats, flew instantly into a rage.

"Out! Out! Just wait till I get hold of you!"

Napolina was slow to her feet. The priest would have caught her, but Monacello scurried into his path: Bad Luck, ugly, mischievous scary little Monacello,

in his black cap, pale eyes flashing with temper. The priest
leapt back with a gasp. "Devil, Monacello!" he said and
promptly tripped over a cat.

The children washed out of the church on a flood of
cats. "What are you waiting for?" called Napolina when
Monacello lagged behind.

"I wanted to say goodbye to the blue lady, but she seems
to have gone."

"Say hello to me instead," said Napolina decidedly.

CHAPTER SEVEN

NAPOLINA

Monacello took Napolina to the Undercity. Proudly he showed her the presents people had left out for him.

"They must like you very much," she said.

"No. They just want me to go away."

He told her about the funny tricks he played on people, but she did not laugh. She did not even smile. He offered her the beads and coins and shiny buttons from his Treasury, but she did not want them.

He told her about the Frezza boys and the boot that had knocked him down the well. Napolina only asked about the boot: "Where is it now?"

"I don't know! Why?"

"Because someone with a hole in his sole might be happy to have a new boot."

Her smile was as sad as a wilted flower, and though she wore layers and layers of clothes, Napolina was always cold. The sun painted on the wall did not warm her.

He could have offered her loneliness, but she already had that. He could have told her his sad life story, but she had enough sadness of her own. He could have offered her unkindness, but she had already eaten too much of that. Only when he brought her the littlest kitten, sleeping curled up in his red cap, did a twinkle glimmer in her dark Neapolitan eyes.

She took the kitten in her arms, but gave Monacello back the cap. "Wear this one today," she said, "for luck." Her hands touching his were cold as ice.

"What kind of luck?"

"Well, good luck, of course! And take a florin with you."

CHAPTER EIGHT

GOOD LUCK BOY

The florin was not the first present Monacello gave away. Before he left the Undercity, Monacello gave one of his woollen robes to Napolina. "You will be warmer now," he said. And oddly, as she put it on, Monacello felt warmer, too.

That evening, the lanes and alleys were alive with rumour. The fleas on the dogs were jumping with the news.

"Old Man Scontroso dropped his last penny in the street, looked round, and found a florin instead! Such luck!"

"… just a moment after he bumped into the Little Monk too!"

"But isn't Monacello …?"

"My pram would have rolled into the river for sure if it hadn't hit that bollard!"

"That was no bollard. That was the Little Monk!"

"But isn't he …?"

"My little grandson had a terrible fever, and dreamed he met Monacello. By morning the fever was gone!"

"But I thought the Little Monk was dead."

"Quite!"

Then a gambler recalled how he had won on a horse called "Monk's Mount". The girl whose sweetheart came home from the sea, remembered glimpsing (as she ran to greet him) an ugly little devil in a red cap.

"Doesn't Monacello wear a black cap?"

"Only when he's making mischief."

That evening, on his way home, scurrying through the shadows, Monacello heard someone call his name. He covered his head and ducked, expecting a flowerpot or a shoe to come flying at his head.

"Hey there! Monacello? Touch my gate, will you? I could do with some luck!"

"So! They think I can bring Good Luck!" Monacello told the cats swarming around his ankles: lucky black cats. "They think I'm lucky, like you. And maybe I AM!" So he put on Good Luck, like a little lambswool robe and it felt soft and cosy. He could not wait to tell Napolina.

"Napolina! Napolina?"

But down in the Undercity, in the room with the sun painted on the wall, her bed was empty. The girl with the sky blue patch over her heart had gone.

CHAPTER NINE

A TERRIBLE MISTAKE

And this is why.

Without the red cap, the littlest kitten had nowhere to sleep. It curled up on Napolina's chest, but the girl's cough made her bumpy. So away went the kitten to join the bigger cats on their nightly prowl.

"Don't go!" Napolina called out to the tip of its tail. "You are too small for the big black night." And when it did not believe her, she went after it. The littlest cat pattered up flues and drains, along dangerous alleys and through gruesome graveyards, along window sills and gutters, roof ridges and church walls. Napolina followed, because there is not much room for luck inside one tiny kitten.

Now Monacello knew every hidden route through
the poor lanes and alleys of Naples. Here he had played
an unkind trick; there he had hidden from the Frezzas.
Yonder he had searched for his mother … The friendly
Moon knew him and helped him search for Napolina.

"Let's hope I am Good Luck Boy tonight!" he told the
Moon, and pulled his red cap hard over his ears. The cats
helped too, a swathe of darkness washing through the city.

The littlest cat pattered across the parapet of the bridge.
Far below, the Sebeto River gleamed silver. High above,
the Moon turned pale. For now, too, a tiny, ragged figure
climbed on to the rail of the bridge, balancing there above
the rushing water. And the Moon had seen more.

The Frezza brothers, full of wine, pointing their fingers,
came barging down the street chanting, "Demon Boy!
Demon Boy die!"

They were mistaken, of course. It was not Monacello
they were seeing there on the bridge, but Napolina,

wearing her warm woollen gift.

From a roof top, Monacello saw the Frezza brothers closing in, saw their mistake, saw their hate. Why such hate? Saw the wine jug fly.

"NO!"

"That's for your mother who brought trouble on us all!"

Without a splash, Napolina fell into the river below. Such a tiny girl.

"NO!"

The Frezzas looked up at the roof, saw a shape like a question mark, and their big mouths fell open. How could Monacello be in two places at once? How could they knock him into the river and then look up and see him? In terror, they picked up their big feet and ran.

Only then did people spill from their houses, hands in their hair, to gape down over the bridge rail. Soon Monacello was beside them.

"Good Luck Boy, don't let the child drown!" And they reached out to him with hopeful hands. But if they wanted to touch him for luck, they were too late. Monacello had leapt from the bridge into the river below.

Questions roared in his head almost as loud as the water, as he plunged down deep and the waves closed over him: Did I bring her this Bad Luck? Am I lucky enough to save her?

The last the people saw of him was his red cap, bobbing in the dark river.

CHAPTER TEN

ONLY MONACELLO

Beneath him, loose slick mud and clutching weed. Above him, the air.

Monacello surfaced and started to swim to and fro, looking for Napolina. He swam downstream, tumbled over a weir. Big, echoey pipes drained rain into the river. As the river swept him along, Monacello shouted into the pipes: "Napolina!" so that every well in the city called up at the sky, "NAPOLINA!"

People said, next day, that the water in the wells tasted of salt, and that horses could not drink without tears filling their blue-brown eyes.

It's hard to swim in a woollen robe, harder still in several. So Monacello swam out of those dark habits of his: Lonely, Frightening, Wicked, Ugly … until only Monacello remained, a cap in each hand: one red, one black. A darkness of empty wool swam alongside him in the current.

Weary, wearily, he floated on down the river and was washed out into the bay, past ships as big as islands and islands the shape of ships, past rocking rowing boats rolling on the swell. The night city rose up like a watching face crowned in a tiara of lights.

He did not wish his cat friends were there with him, piled on his chest, making him warm. Cats are afraid of water, and he did not want his friends to be afraid. He did not want anyone to share the fear pounding in his thin, little chest. He realised, with a pang of sorrow, that he had never asked Napolina what frightened her. He had never asked her the who, how, where and when of her own ragged life. And now she was gone! A blue patch of sky, the exact same colour Napolina wore, made his eyes prickle with tears…

Geraldine McCaughrean

Then dawn: a single patch of blue over the heart of the
sky. And there on a wave-top, rising and falling like a

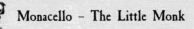

kitten on a sleeper's chest: Napolina. He would never have seen her but for the white stillness of her floating hands.

Outside the city lay fields where sheep strayed and frayed the grass. There were orchards, too, hung with the golden globes of oranges, the silver sheen of pomegranates, the happy bubble of purple grapes.

Monacello and Napolina danced in honey-golden sunshine, wearing smiles as white as Neapolitan ice cream, eating olives from the littlest trees. From so far away, the city, rising steeply out of the sea, was beautiful: you would have to have gone much closer to see the bits of darkness caught on all its sharp corners.

"Will you go back?" asked Napolina, "or run away to sea and beyond?"

The bright sea sparkled with promise. The little boats in the bay tugged at their mooring ropes, wanting to be gone.

But the big booming bells of the city were calling him: "MOnaceLLO! MOnaceLLO!" The Undercity was rumbling with emptiness. The city was daring him to stay.

"The Frezzas know something about my mother."

"I know," said Napolina. "Memory sleeps on their chests. It has sharp claws. That's why they hate you." It was as if she had known all along.

"I'm going to find her. Will you help me look?"

"Yes," said Napolina, "even when you cannot see me." (Which was an odd thing to say, because Monacello did not miss much with his pale, peculiar eyes). Her hand on his arm was so warm and light now that he could barely feel it. There was a smell in her hair of purple smoke, and beyond her eyes the glimmer of candle flames.

In the poorest district, people were opening their shutters on a new day. Some caught a glimpse as he passed: a little hooded monk dressed in a dark robe, a soggy cap dripping from each hand, one red, one black. Monacello heard parents call their children indoors: anxious, scolding voices. "Quick! I think I just saw Monacello!"

Others cursed and spat. "May he keep his bad luck to himself!"

Now and then, though, he heard a different, whispered wish:

"Bring me a sweetheart, Monacello."

"Let me find work, Monacello."

"Make Mama well, Monacello."

Once a pebble hit him: "Go Away, Jinx!" But once some flower petals from a window box landed on his hair: "Bring me good luck, Monacello!"

As he scurried past the Villa Frezza, his small heart quaked with fear, but it could not be helped: Naples was home. Somewhere inside it grew a story, planted before he

was born; his story.

He would not stop looking till he found it.

A long morning shadow of cats fell in behind him.

And Napolina, too

(though he did not see her).

BOOK II

THE WISH–BRINGER

Amid the strangers and dangers of Naples,
lies the secret Monacello longs to find.
Perhaps it will explain why the Frezza brothers
hate him so much.
Perhaps it will find him a home closer to the sunshine,
a bedcover less dusty and with fewer fleas.

Is he brave enough for the truth?
Some secrets are so terrible it may be better not to know.
Of course! King of the Undercity? Of course he is brave!
In the meantime, all Naples peeps through its shutters,
watching for Monacello, the Good-Luck, Bad-Luck Boy.